CHIMNEY CHILD

A Victorian Story

By Laurie Sheehan

Illustrated by Gillian Marklew

ANGLIA *young* BOOKS

First published in 1998
by Anglia Young Books
Durhams Farmhouse
Ickleton
Saffron Walden, Essex CB10 1SR

Illustrations by Gillian Marklew

British Library Cataloguing-in-Publication Data

A catalogue record for this book is available from the
British Library

ISBN 1 871173 57 4

Typeset in Palatino by Goodfellow & Egan, Cambridge
and printed in Great Britain by Ashford Colour Press,
Gosport, Hampshire

CHAPTER ONE

Sam Ruff, the chimney sweep, was standing by the fire in the kitchen of a large London house.

Beside him stood the new climbing boy, Vic, rubbing his eyes with his grubby fists. He was a thin child of about eight and he was trying hard not to cry.

Sam Ruff pushed the boy nearer the fire but Vic squirmed away and flattened himself against the far wall.

'Please, Mr Ruff! Please don't do it again!'

Sam Ruff lost patience. He raised his cane and lashed out at Vic.

'Do as I say, curse you!' he shouted. 'You'll thank me in the end, you little fool. If you want to be a climbing boy, you have to have hard skin on your knees.'

'I don't mind if my knees bleed,' whispered Vic.

'Well, I do,' said Ruff. Then he turned towards the door into the passage, where the butler was standing impassively. Ruff pointed to the man.

'What do you think the Browne family would think if you left blood over their fine furnishings? What do you think the butler would tell them?'

Vic swallowed. 'Please,' he repeated. But even as he said it, he knew that he would have to give in.

Ruff pushed him close up to the flames again and, still holding him, bent down and dipped a filthy rag into a bowl of strong brine. He began rubbing the salty water into Vic's bleeding knees.

Vic's eyes watered with pain but he bit his lip and forced himself not to cry out. Would it never end? He felt as though his knees were on fire and he hardly heard Ruff's voice.

'You're a slow worker, Vic. You've only done one chimney in this house and that was the easy one, the short, wide one. You still have to climb that long, narrow chimney in the main bedroom. And then we've got two more big houses to do here in the City today.'

Vic was dimly aware that someone else had joined the butler at the kitchen door. It was a boy. A boy a couple of years older than Vic and much taller. He was dressed in a smart green velvet suit and his eyes widened as he watched the scene beside the fire.

The older boy turned to the butler and pulled at his sleeve.

'Jackson, what's the man doing?'

'No need for you to concern yourself, Master Albert,' said the butler. 'No doubt the chimney sweep knows his business.'

Albert winced as the sweep continued to rub at Vic's inflamed knees.

'If Mamma or Papa were here, they wouldn't allow such cruelty,' he said gruffly. 'I'm going to put a stop to this.'

But as Albert lunged forward, Jackson

grabbed his arm and said sharply, 'Leave him be, Master Albert. Your parents have left me in charge this afternoon and it's not our place to interfere.'

At that moment, Sam Ruff let go of Vic and stood up.

'That'll do for now,' he said. 'We've wasted enough time already. We must get upstairs.' Turning to Jackson and Albert, he addressed them for the first time.

'If I were you, I'd stay away from the bedroom. The chimney's narrow and twisting and there'll be a good deal of soot.'

'I'd like to watch,' said Albert stubbornly. He had the feeling that the chimney boy might be better treated if he was in the room.

Ruff looked him up and down, observing Albert's velvet suit and fresh clean linen. He gave a mirthless laugh.

'Oh no, young master,' he said. 'That wouldn't do at all.'

Albert blushed, suddenly feeling ashamed of his smart clothes.

'He's right, Master Albert,' said Jackson. 'You

should stay in your room. You're excused lessons because of that bad cough; you don't want to inflame it with soot.'

Sam Ruff and Vic carried the brooms, brushes and an empty sack up to the main bedroom. The stairs and the bedroom were shrouded in sheets to protect the carpets and furniture.

Jackson and Albert followed from the kitchen. At the foot of the stairs, the butler turned to the boy.

'Don't worry, Master Albert,' he whispered. 'I'll keep an eye on them. All sweeps are thieves and we don't want your mamma to come home and find some of her jewellery missing.'

Albert hesitated. But he knew that his parents would be angry if he disobeyed Jackson, so he did as he was told and went to his room.

So while Vic wriggled and squeezed his way up the chimney, Albert sat next door. He shivered. The River Thames was nearby. The fog was closing in and the room was damp. But his own chimney joined the one in the main bedroom. There could be no fire in his room until the climbing boy had done his job.

He found his new book. It was called

'*The Arabian Nights*' and his parents had given it to him for his birthday last week. 'Albert Browne. On the occasion of his tenth birthday. From his loving parents. 1st October, 1873.'

Soon Albert was engrossed in his book and forgot all about the terrified chimney child.

But before long, some of the soot seeped under the door and into his room.

Albert began to cough. The rasping cough which had so worried his mother that she'd told his tutor to cancel today's lessons.

His eyes watered. He tried to take some deep breaths, but still he couldn't stop coughing.

The door opened and Jackson came in.

'Are you all right, Master Albert?'

Albert tried to speak but was overwhelmed by another spasm of coughing.

Jackson crossed to the washstand and poured some water from the jug into a glass. He returned to Albert and offered it to him. The boy took it thankfully.

'Drink it slowly, Master Albert.'

Albert did as he was told and at last the spasm passed.

'Thank you, Jackson,' he said. 'I'm better now. It was just the soot.'

Jackson waited a little longer, then replaced the glass and went back to the door.

'Are you quite recovered, Master Albert?'

Albert nodded. 'Quite.'

Jackson smiled at him. 'Good. Then I'd better go back to those two stinking gutter-rats next door.'

Albert didn't smile back.

Some time later, he heard the door slam in the main bedroom and the sound of voices and footsteps going down the stairs.

'Thank heaven,' he thought. 'Now at last I can have a fire again.'

He got up and stretched. He heard the front door close.

Then he heard Jackson climbing the stairs again and going into the main bedroom to remove the dust-sheets from the furniture.

Suddenly there was a yell.

Albert opened his bedroom door and looked out.

'Jackson? Jackson, what's the matter?'

Jackson emerged from the main bedroom, looking furious.

'The thieving beggars!' he yelled.

'What's happened?'

'They've stolen your mother's small jewel-box, Master Albert. That's what's happened.'

'But you were there with them, weren't you?' said Albert. 'You were watching them.'

'Most of the time I was. But there were those few minutes when I heard you coughing and came in to give you the water.'

'Of course,' said Albert. 'And you think it was then?'

'It must have been,' said Jackson. 'Oh dear, it's all my fault. What will your parents say? They trusted me to look after things. I've only been here a couple of weeks and already I've let them down.'

'It's not your fault, Jackson,' said Albert. Then he ran over to the landing window.

'Look. They haven't got far. Let's give chase!'

For a second Jackson hesitated.

Then he said, 'Yes. Yes! We'll catch them redhanded.'

They rushed down the stairs, through the hall and out of the front door into the foggy street. Sam Ruff and Vic were trailing along the pavement.

Jackson reached them first. He grabbed Sam by the shoulder.

'Stop thief!' he shouted.

Sam Ruff spun round.

'Don't you accuse me of thieving, mister high and mighty butler,' he said. 'I'd be a fool to thieve from those who give me work.'

Jackson was panting hard. 'There's no other explanation,' he said. 'Mrs Browne's jewel-box was on the dressing-table when I covered the furniture and now it's gone.'

'But you were there!' shouted Sam. 'You were with us all the time.'

'No I wasn't,' said Jackson. 'I went to tend Master Albert when I heard him coughing. I was out of the room for several minutes.'

'But I. . .'

'And,' said Jackson, 'when I returned, the boy had come down the chimney and was standing by the dressing-table.'

Ruff stared at Vic.

'You thieving little rat,' he yelled. 'What have you done with it?'

Vic began to tremble. 'I didn't take it,' he murmured. 'I didn't.'

'Lying little cur,' roared Ruff, raising his cane. 'Is it down your shirt? Tell me where you've put it or I'll beat you till your whole body bleeds, not just your knees and elbows.'

But Vic didn't wait to hear any more. He darted between the men's legs and ran as he had never run before.

CHAPTER TWO

Vic was so terrified that he hardly felt his sore knees. He ran into the thickening fog with Ruff, Jackson and Albert close on his heels. His pursuers' cries soon merged into other sounds: ships' foghorns and curses from angry drivers, as he dodged past horses' hoofs and headed for the Thames.

Soon he was slithering down a muddy alley between huge fenced-off warehouses.

Some way behind, Albert felt his chest tightening as he raced after the chimney child. But he wasn't going to let him escape.

'To think that I felt sorry for the brat,' he thought.

Ahead of him, Jackson and Ruff had suddenly stopped. They were standing beside a nine-foot fence.

Albert ran up to them. 'What's happened? Where is he?'

Jackson pointed to a hole at the bottom of the fence.

'He's wriggled through there, rot him.'

Sam Ruff sighed. 'We'll never catch him now.' He looked around him. 'The fog's closing in and by the time we've found a way round this fence, he'll have vanished.'

'Little rat,' said Jackson, nodding in agreement. 'He'll be able to hide up in the grain sheds. We'll never find him now.'

Albert looked at the hole. The men would never be able to squeeze through, it was true, but perhaps *he* could.

While Ruff and Jackson paced up and down the fence, Albert got down on all fours and squeezed his head and shoulders through the hole. He heard the cloth of his suit rip and then he heard Jackson's voice.

'What are you doing, Master Albert? Come

back. You shouldn't be out in this fog. Your cough! Come back, Master Albert.'

Albert ignored him. He could think of nothing except getting back his mother's jewels. The climbing boy was small and ill-fed. He'd soon tire. If Albert could find him, he could overpower him.

With one more shove, he was through the fence and the sound of Jackson's shouts grew fainter.

Albert walked away from the fence and down towards the river. All noises were muffled by the thick fog and the silence was eerie.

Suddenly there was a scuffling noise and Albert jumped. Was it a rat? A boy?

'Hey, is that you, you thief?' His voice sounded strange and unnatural.

There was a scrambling and then Albert saw a shadowy form climbing up a stack of barrels near a locked gate. The climbing boy! Albert ran towards him but already Vic had swarmed over the gate and leapt down to the other side.

Albert, too, scrambled up the barrels and, giving himself no time to think, he jumped from the top of the gate into the fog.

He landed awkwardly, twisting his ankle, and couldn't help crying out with pain, but he forced himself to go on. Vic was ahead of him, slithering down some slimy stone steps to the Thames mud.

Albert limped towards the steps. By now, Vic had disappeared into the fog. Albert peered through the gloom.

Nothing.

He stood on the top step. By straining his eyes, he could just make out the boy's retreating form, farther along the mud.

As Albert edged his way down, two much more threatening figures suddenly loomed from the fog. Two big boys. They'd picked up something from the mud at the water's edge and were squelching towards him.

Mudlarks! He'd often seen mudlarks when riding in his father's carriage.

'Hey,' said one, his ragged clothes stiff with dried mud. 'Look at this lovely suit. If we stripped it off him and sold it, we could buy pie and mash for a month.'

Terrified, Albert turned to run, but he lost his footing and slipped.

He fell into the mud. He tried to pull himself out but he was stuck.

And he was sinking.

The mudlarks turned their backs on him and wandered off. They'd return shortly when he couldn't struggle.

Desperately, Albert looked around him. Fog. Just fog.

'Help,' he shouted. 'Someone help me.'

There was no answer and Albert struggled some more. But the more he did, the worse it got.

'Help!' he yelled again. 'I'm sinking!'

Then suddenly there was someone beside him and a hand grasped his.

It was the chimney child!

But Albert's fingers were numb with cold and Vic wasn't strong enough to pull him free.

He had to let go.

'Don't leave me!' cried Albert. He floundered

in panic and sank lower in the mud. By now it was up to his waist.

'I'm going to find a plank,' said Vic. 'Though God alone knows why I should bother to help you.'

Vic squelched over to a plank he'd seen floating among the sewage at the water's edge. He dragged it back to Albert and shoved the end against his chest, then he knelt on the wood.

'Grab my hand,' said Vic, 'and try to heave yourself onto the plank.'

It was agonizingly slow but gradually they managed it. At last Albert lay, stinking and covered with mud, full length on the plank.

By now the mudlarks had heard the boys' voices and were returning. They didn't want to lose their prize. Even if the suit was ruined, there'd be rich pickings in the pockets.

Vic spotted the pair first. 'Hurry, Albert! Get up and run. Come on, follow me.'

Vic guided him towards some more steps. It seemed to take ages. The mud slowed them but at last they had climbed the steps and were running along a riverside path.

Albert stopped for a moment to catch his breath. 'Have they gone?' he asked fearfully.

Vic shrugged. 'I don't know. But we'd better keep going. They know every inch of the riverside.'

They ran on blindly for a long while, often stumbling with exhaustion, the constant foghorns telling them that they were still close to the water.

When they felt boards under their feet, Vic stopped.

'Where are we?' asked Albert.

'On a quay,' said Vic. Then he pointed to a long, low shape beneath them.

'What's that?' asked Albert.

'A coal-barge. It's a good place to hide. We'll jump down.'

Albert had been so terrified that he'd forced himself to run on his injured ankle. But now that he'd stopped running, he realized how badly it was hurt. Also he was covered in mud and his chest was tight and painful.

Vic helped him down and they crept in among the coals on the barge.

Albert started to shiver. He couldn't help it.

'I'm so cold,' he said. 'We can't stay here all night, Vic.'

'It's getting dark and it's so foggy now, we'll have to. Anyway, I'm used to sleeping out.'

Albert, who had never before missed a night in his warm bed, was horrified.

'But how can you do it?' he asked, still shivering uncontrollably.

'I've never known anything else. It's either that or the workhouse and I'd rather be free.' Then Vic sighed. 'But lately I've been starving, so that's why I asked Sam Ruff for work. At least he would have given me some bread and let me sleep in his cellar.'

'Where are your parents?'

Vic turned away. 'They died of the cholera when I was a baby. The doctor said it was because they drank Thames water.'

'So who cared for you after they'd died?'

'My brother.'

'You're lucky to have a brother,' said Albert. 'I don't have a brother, or a sister.'

Vic said nothing. He shuffled himself farther down into the coal.

'My brother and I were mudlarks, too,' he said, 'but on a different part of the river. We used to look in the mud for coal and bones and rags to sell. If we found copper nails, we'd get fourpence a pound.'

Albert was silent for a while.

Then he said, 'If you'd got a job, Vic, why did you steal my mother's jewels?'

Vic sat up. 'I did NOT steal them. I swear to you I didn't steal them, Albert. I don't know who did, but I swear it wasn't me. Feel my shirt.'

Albert did so. There was nothing there. Again, he remained silent.

Vic went on, 'I suppose Mr Ruff may have taken them when I wasn't looking and then blamed me. He said I was a slow climbing boy, so I don't suppose he'll mind losing me if he can keep the jewels.'

Albert nodded into the gathering darkness. 'I believe you, Vic,' he said.

Neither of them spoke for a long time. Night had come and the fog and the sound of the water surrounded them.

'Vic,' said Albert at last, 'what will you do now? Will you go back to your brother?'

Vic squirmed in the coal but said nothing. Later, Albert heard a sniff.

'You're not crying, are you, Vic? I thought all you ragged children were as hard as copper nails.'

There was another sniff and then Vic said, in a whisper, 'My brother died of consumption a few weeks ago.' Then added crossly, 'A girl's allowed to cry for her dead brother, isn't she?'

Albert sat bolt upright. 'A *girl*! What are you talking about?'

Vic cursed loudly.

'I didn't mean to tell you. But you might as well know the truth, I suppose.'

'You're a *girl*!'

'Yes. I had to pretend to be a boy in case Sam Ruff wouldn't give me a job.'

'So. . .. what's your real name, then?'

Vic sniffed. 'Vic. Victoria Wells, at your service.'

CHAPTER THREE

Morning came and the fog was just as thick. Albert's cough had spread to his chest and his ankle was swollen.

'I'll never be able to get home,' he gasped. 'I can hardly breathe now and my ankle hurts terribly. *You* know your way about London blindfold. The fog won't stop you. Please, Vic, will you fetch my father?'

'I wouldn't dare go back to that big house!' cried Vic. 'Your father wouldn't believe I didn't steal the jewel-box.'

'Papa would listen to you; I know he would.'

'Of course he wouldn't,' said Vic. 'Why would a rich banker man like him listen to a little sweep like me?'

'Because he's a Christian gentleman, Vic,' said Albert, feeling himself getting weaker.

'He'd have me thrown into Newgate, soon as listen to me. I couldn't bear that. I must be free. I'd die in there.'

'Papa's a fair man and kind. He and his friend Mr Barclay and other Christian bankers are always having meetings in our house. They're forever talking about their charity work, and worrying about street children, and the poor dying of consumption, and...' Albert's strength had almost gone. 'He wouldn't just condemn you as a thief because you're a stinking sweep. He'd listen to your story. Please, Vic.'

'I can't,' she mumbled. 'I'd be terrified.'

'Please!'

Albert collapsed, exhausted.

She gasped. 'Albert, are you all right?'

There was no reply, only a terrible coughing. It reminded Vic of her brother, just before he'd died.

She shook Albert gently, but he only moaned.

She didn't know *what* to do. Her brother had died of consumption, Mr Browne wanted to help such people, and now his own son would also die in this horrible way because *she* was too scared to help him.

At last, she came to a decision.

'All right, Albert, I'll try to find your father,' she said, then clambered up the side of the barge.

Soon Vic had left Albert and the barge far behind and was following the river again, back to the City. It was a long way to walk and her legs ached with cold and weariness. The slightest sound set her nerves twitching; she knew that despite the fog, the police would be looking for Albert and the thief who'd lured him away. After all, he was a rich man's son.

There'd be less chance of getting caught if she kept to the maze of alleys. She entered one, feeling her way along the side of a low wall. She gasped as something squealed and brushed past her bare arm. A rat!

She wanted to get away from this neighbourhood as soon as possible. It was the largest criminal quarter of London. No one suffered more from the brutal thieves around here than the poor themselves. Such rogues would steal a halfpenny from a hungry child looking in a cook-shop window, and knock the victim into the gutter. Being dockland, it was also the haunt of sailors and bad women and girls.

But she couldn't walk any faster.

Her elbow was grabbed.

'Well, hello!' A man's voice, thick with drink.

Snatching her arm away, she fled.

Half an hour later, she was still in dockland. By using the alleys, she was taking twice as long as she should. All that she wanted to do was lie down and sleep.

Snatches of conversation reached her from the street ahead.

'Look in barrels . . . under arches . . . tarpaulin . . . Search the alleys.'

Vic stiffened. The police! Turning round, she went quickly back the way she'd come.

Then she entered yet another alley. Ahead two men were talking, their voices muffled by

the fog. She had to go on, though. She couldn't go back and be caught by the police.

Unnoticed by the two men, she slipped inside a doorway. It was dark in the alley and the fog swirled around her but she could just make out the forms of the men. One was tall and the other much shorter. The tall man was handing something to the smaller one in return for money.

There was some more conversation and then the smaller man vanished into a doorway and she heard the door creak shut. The taller fellow started to walk away. Vic moved slightly and the tall man turned back sharply. It was then that Vic saw his face and, even in the dim, fog-bound alley, she recognized him!

He walked on. Before Vic had gathered her wits, he was at the top of the alley and turning left, towards the City. She ran after him.

But when she reached the street, there was no sign of him.

'Well, well, well, what do we have here?'

Vic swung round to face a policeman.

She had to think quickly.

'Don't slow me down, mister. I'm in a rush to fetch Mum from work. My baby brother's been taken ill because of the fog.'

'Where does your mother work?' he asked.

'Er – at Bow matchworks.'

'But that's two miles away. You'll never find it in this fog. Goodness, you don't half stink of soot! You're a sweep.'

'No I'm not. I got messed up, cleaning Mum's grate.'

He dragged her under the feeble light of a gas-lamp.

'I thought so,' he said. 'You're a sweep all right. And your age and height match the description of the one who stole the jewels from Mr Browne the banker's house and lured away his boy. And your name's Vic, isn't it?'

It was hopeless. 'Yes,' she mumbled.

'The police all over London have been looking for you, my lad.'

'But I didn't steal the jewels. I rescued. . .'

'Quiet, you lying brat! You're under arrest. You'll soon be in Newgate Prison.' He whirled his rattle to call his colleagues.

CHAPTER FOUR

It hurt to breathe. Vic had been gone for hours and the fog had finally lifted. Albert's thoughts kept drifting to *'The Arabian Nights'*. He was flying away on a magic carpet. He moved his leg and a pain shot through his ankle, bringing him back to earth.

He'd die if he stayed here.

'Help!' he cried feebly. 'Somebody help me!'

The only response was the mocking cry of a seagull.

If he piled up some more coal, perhaps he could climb out. It was so loose, though, it wouldn't be easy to pile or to climb.

The quicker he piled, the quicker the

wretched stuff fell down. But, at last, with his strength almost gone, he'd finished.

Twice he slid down. But at his third try, he managed to crawl right up.

Once on the quay, he found a length of wood to use as a crutch.

Soon he was limping through the East End streets. What a sight he was, covered in mud – like a stinking gutter-rat. He no longer looked like a boy of his own class and he was really scared. He'd be thrown into the workhouse!

A coal-wagon was rattling towards him.

'Out of the road, you plaguy mudlark!' roared the black-faced coalman, raising his whip.

Albert ducked just in time.

Three youths with jail-cropped heads and flashy, threadbare clothes were hanging about at the far end of the cobbled street. He staggered to the opposite side. But as he drew level, they ran across and poked him with sticks.

'Cor, strike a light!' cried the biggest of the three. 'He stinks worse than you two did when we were in prison.'

The smallest jabbed him extra hard and he fell to the cobbles. Then the youths ran off, laughing.

Two gentlemen with canes were hurrying past as he pulled himself up to sit against a horse-trough. They looked like bankers and might have known his father but Albert didn't have the strength to speak.

'Ugh! What a disgusting creature!' said one, holding his nose.

'He'd be better for a wash in the trough,' said the other.

Finally, using the trough and his 'crutch', Albert managed to get back onto his unsteady feet. The pavement was moving!

He knew that he was about to faint but somehow he reached the next street. And the next. And even the next. Though, hadn't he been in this one before? Everything was so muzzy, as if the fog had returned.

Hardly able to make out the sign, he saw that he was now in a narrow, squalid street called Stepney Causeway. He clutched some railings round a large terraced house. As he swung there, his eyes caught some words painted on a board above the ground-floor windows of this house and the one next door:

NO DESTITUTE CHILD
EVER REFUSED ADMISSION

There was a brass plate on the panelling inside the porch. By gripping the side-railings, he succeeded in pulling himself up the three steps to peer at the words.

BOYS' HOME.
HONORARY DIRECTOR: T. J. BARNARDO

Dr Thomas Barnardo was the man whom Albert's parents had visited yesterday. That's where they'd been when Sam Ruff and Vic came to sweep the chimneys. The doctor wanted money from Browne's Bank to open a home for girls.

'Help me, someone!' cried Albert, punching the door. 'Help me!'

There was a clattering of wheels and a horse neighed. A hansom cab stopped and a short young gentleman in a black greatcoat alighted. He wore a top hat and spectacles, and his brown side-whiskers were long and fluffy.

'Oh, my poor lad!' he gasped. 'What a state

you're in!' The accent was Irish. He lifted the knocker, striking smartly three times, then turned to the cab-driver, who'd climbed down. 'Help me carry him inside.'

'Yes, Dr Barnardo,' said the cabby. 'God love us, this must be the hundredth mudlark you've rescued.'

As they lifted Albert between them, the door swung open.

'I'm no stinking mudlark,' protested Albert. 'I'm a banker's son. I'm. . .'

'Yeah, and I'm a monkey's uncle,' grunted the cabby, leading the way into the hall.

Dr Barnardo was studying Albert's clothes.

'There's velvet under all this mud,' he said thoughtfully.

'I told you,' croaked Albert. 'I'm Albert Browne, son of Mr Browne of Browne's Bank.'

They laid him on a bench and the doctor examined him more closely.

'And his hair is neatly cut and his nails are short.'

Barnardo undid Albert's top pocket and took

out a damp but mud-free diary. He opened it and read aloud the pencilled words.

'"This diary belongs to Albert Browne . . ." Praise the Lord you're safe!' he cried.

The cab-driver was smiling now. 'Half of London has been looking for you after that little thief lured you away,' he said. 'All of us cabbies have been on a sharp lookout. They've taken the boy to Newgate and it serves him right.'

'Vic's not a thief,' whispered Albert. 'She saved my life. We must get. . ..'

He couldn't manage the words. The ceiling above the doctor's face was darkening, his features blurring, and then there was nothing.

When Albert came round, he found himself in a hard bed, one of a dozen in a small dormitory. The sun was shining on whitewashed walls covered with religious pictures and texts. The mud had been washed from him and he was wearing a woollen nightshirt. Dr Barnardo himself held his hand and he looked worried.

'You were too sick to move, Albert, so I've sent for your parents.'

There was a knock on the door.

'Ah, I think this is them now,' said the doctor.

Albert's mother rushed in. She came to his bedside, held him in her arms and sobbed.

His father followed. 'Oh, my poor boy!' he cried. 'What a terrible time you've had! Jackson has told us everything. He says that you were trying to catch that little rascal who stole your mother's jewels. It was a brave thing to do, Albert, but stupid, too.'

'Vic didn't steal the jewels, Papa. It must have been Sam Ruff. Vic saved my life in the mud. Then she kept me safe for the night in a coalbarge. She was going to you for help but someone said that she'd been taken to Newgate. We must get her out. Vic is used to being free. She'll die in there!'

'She?' said his father. 'She? What are you talking about? The sweep's a boy. You're delirious, son. Now get some sleep. You'll be more your old self in the morning.'

'I'm not delirious, Papa. It's all true!'

Albert's mother wiped his brow with a damp cloth. 'Go to sleep, dear,' she said, kissing his cheek.

His strength was going. Despite his efforts to stay awake, he was drifting back to sleep.

* * *

He had lost track of time. He was feeling much better, though. His parents and Dr Barnardo were with him again.

'How long have I been lying here?'

'Five days, Albert,' said Dr Barnardo. 'You're over the worst of your illness. Your dear parents are taking you home today.'

'I want to go to Newgate first. Poor Vic. Five days!'

'Don't be silly, Albert,' said his mother. 'Papa and I don't want you to have anything more to do with that horrid thief.'

'She's not a thief. I've already told you.'

Albert's father turned to Dr Barnardo. 'Oh dear. He still seems very muddled.' Then he said patiently: 'The sweep is not a girl, Albert.'

'She is. She is!' Albert coughed violently. 'Why won't anyone believe me?'

'Because you're talking nonsense, darling,' said his mother softly. 'Did anyone ever hear of a climbing *girl*?'

'I tell you, she *is*!' cried Albert, exhausting himself.

His father's cheeks reddened. 'That's enough of your nonsense, Albert.'

Dr Barnardo put his hand on Mr Browne's sleeve. 'The lad's right, sir. Even though all the little sweeps are known as climbing *boys*, some are, indeed, girls.'

'What?' he gasped. 'But – but this is terrible!'

'Yes, it is,' said the doctor. 'But I can assure you it's true. I have come across some climbing girls during my nightly searches for London's waifs.'

'Please believe me, Papa,' said Albert, easing himself out of bed. 'And please let me go to Newgate to find her.'

Dr Barnardo and Mr Browne exchanged glances.

The doctor said quietly, 'If Albert is so determined to see the child, then perhaps we should go to Newgate.'

There was a long silence. Albert looked from his parents to Dr Barnardo.

'Very well,' said Mr Browne at last. 'Will you accompany us in the carriage, Dr Barnardo?'

On the way to Newgate, Albert told his parents and Dr Barnardo, as calmly as he could, all that had happened. It was only a couple of miles but the journey tired him. At last, they arrived outside the grim soot-blackened prison in the Old Bailey, at the spot where public hangings had ended just five years ago.

They were let in and, after long delays caused by the unlocking of countless gates, finally brought to Vic's small, dark cell.

Clutching its slimy wall for support, Albert stared at her. She was lying so still, on a thin mattress, on the asphalt floor. She had been so full of life when he'd last seen her. Just five days in Newgate had caused this.

Her sooty face was streaked with sweat. Her eyes were closed. She was struggling to breathe.

Dr Barnardo turned to Albert. 'This is scandalous! We'll go straight to a magistrate,' he said. 'If you tell him what you've told us, he'll have to free the dear girl. Then we'll have her taken to hospital.'

'Oh, Albert,' said his father, 'I'm sorry, boy. I thought that you were just rambling because of your illness. Look at her, poor child. I'm glad we left your mamma in the carriage. This would have distressed her too much.'

Dr Barnardo addressed the female turnkey. 'Let us out, woman. There's no time for delay.'

* * *

Albert spoke up bravely to the magistrate.

'And so you see, sir,' he said, 'Vic's not a thief at all but a brave girl.'

'She shall be freed at once,' said the elderly gentleman. He wrote something on a sheet of paper, then turned to a policeman. 'Constable Flynn, please arrange for Victoria Wells to be taken to St Bartholomew's Hospital immediately. I shall be asking your superiors to make further enquiries in this case as a matter of urgency. That man Ruff has some questions to answer.'

Some time later, Albert was in Sam Ruff's tumbledown Aldgate house with Constables Flynn and Smith.

'I didn't steal the jewels!' cried Ruff. 'Vic's the thief, not me.'

'We'll search from top to bottom,' said Constable Flynn, a red-faced Irishman.

'Search all you like,' said Ruff. 'But you won't find the jewels here.'

He was right. After a thorough search, the policemen found nothing.

'I told you so,' said Ruff, as they climbed the cellar stairs.

'Where are your sacks of soot?' asked Albert.

'I've sold them to the farmers to spread on their fields.'

'He probably sold the jewels on the day he stole them,' muttered Albert.

'A likely story,' sneered Ruff. 'Do you think I stumbled about London in thick fog? I never even got to the other two houses to clean the chimneys, the fog was so dense.'

He opened the front door to let them out.

'We'll be back,' said Constable Flynn. 'Come on, Albert.'

The boy jumped as Ruff slammed the door behind them.

As they walked away, Albert tugged at Flynn's sleeve.

'Can you take me to see Vic in the hospital, constable?'

Constable Flynn looked doubtful.

'I promised your parents to deliver you safely home,' he said.

'Please! I must see her. It won't take long, I promise!'

Constable Flynn looked down at Albert's anxious face.

He smiled. 'Very well,' he said.

Albert had never been to a hospital. When he entered Vic's ward, he was amazed at its size. And the smell. Everything smelt of carbolic soap.

Vic looked so small in the big bed. She was nearly as white as the sheet. Her eyes were still closed and he couldn't even hear her breathing now. Kneeling by the bed, he held her clammy hand.

'Hello, Vic,' he said. 'It's me: Albert.'

No reply.

'Can you hear me, Vic? Please say you can.'

'Yes,' she whispered with a huge effort, her eyes staying shut.

'Thank goodness,' he said.

'Vic,' he went on, 'I have a policeman with me, Constable Flynn. We've visited Sam Ruff's but haven't found anything Oh, if only you could speak. But I don't want to tire you.'

Her hand squeezed his.

'It *was* Ruff, wasn't it, Vic?'

'No, Albert,' she murmured.

'But there were only you two in the room! Except for Jackson of course. You're not saying that it was Jackson, are you?'

'Yes.'

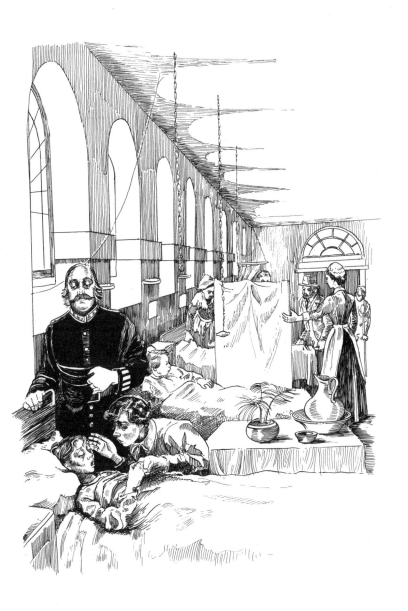

'Jackson! But how do you know? You said before, that you didn't know.'

'Saw him give . . . something to man in alley behind Butcher Row.'

Constable Flynn looked serious. 'A fellow-countryman of mine called Dermot O'Hara has a secondhand-jewellery shop there. But he's also a receiver of stolen property. In fact, he's only recently come out of Newgate.'

'How can he sell them if people can recognize their own jewels?' asked Albert.

'He resets or recuts the gems to disguise them. I think that you and I had better pay a call on Mr O'Hara.'

Albert squeezed Vic's hand. 'I'll be back to see you soon, Vic. Get some sleep now. Goodbye.'

Constable Flynn ruffled her sweat-soaked hair.

'Goodbye, lass. You get yourself better now.'

'Goodbye,' she whispered. And still her eyes stayed shut.

'Let's hope that Mamma's jewels have not been changed and sold already,' said Albert as they hurried from the hospital.

CHAPTER SIX

As Constable Flynn was a City of London policeman, he had no authority outside the 'Square Mile'. So he'd brought along a colleague from the Metropolitan Police.

The dingy shop and its bald-headed owner smelt nearly as bad as Albert had when covered with mud.

'Well, Constable Flynn,' said Dermot O'Hara, 'the boy's seen all my jewels and hasn't recognized one. Now, will you leave a fellow in peace to get on with his lawful business?'

The constable sighed. 'He's right, Albert. If the jewels were here once, they're not now – at least not in their original form. Come on, lad.'

Albert frowned and pointed to a curtain. 'What about in there? Perhaps he has a workshop at the back.'

'I do all my work in here, on the counter,' said the Irishman quickly, putting his watch-maker's glass to his eye. 'Look, here are all my tools, for mending watches and necklaces and the like.'

Albert took no notice. Lifting the counter hatch, he pushed past O'Hara and through the curtain. There was a scuffle as O'Hara tried to dash for the shop door but Constable Flynn grabbed him.

In a room hardly bigger than a broom cupboard was a small workbench cluttered with broken-up jewels. Albert muttered a curse. They were too late!

There was a shelf, though, higher than his head. He felt along it.

Nothing, except cobwebs and thick dust.

Just as thick was the dust on the mat, which covered the whole floor. But if the mat had been lifted recently, the dust would have been disturbed. There'd be finger-marks. Still, it was hard to tell, in the late-afternoon light from the tiny window. His heart pounding, he crouched down and rolled back the mat.

He tested the floorboards with his feet. The short board in the corner was loose! He knelt down and removed it, then felt inside the dark hole. He touched something hard.

He took it out.

A jewel-box just like his mother's!

With trembling fingers, Albert opened it.

'They're here, constable! All the jewels are untouched!'

'It'll be back to Newgate for you, Dermot,' said Flynn. 'Well done, Albert, lad.'

* * *

Jackson the butler was arrested and finally confessed to stealing the jewels.

Two weeks later, Vic left hospital. Dr Barnardo collected her in his cab and they drove to the Brownes' house. All three Brownes were there to greet them.

Sitting beside Vic on the sofa in the huge drawing-room, the doctor smiled reassuringly at her.

'Thanks to you, my dear, Jackson and Sam Ruff are both behind bars now.'

Vic found her voice. 'What d'you mean, sir?' she asked. 'Why is Sam Ruff in prison?'

'He was arrested for using you as a climbing child. It's against the law to use children as sweeps. But there are still at least two thousand other little souls like you, aged mainly between five and ten, who are employed in this barbarous way throughout the country.'

Albert's father joined in. 'If *I* had been here when Ruff brought you to sweep the chimneys, I'd have called the police. It suited Jackson not to, of course.'

Albert laughed. 'I can imagine the scene if Ruff and Jackson share the same cell. They'll tear each other's hair out.'

Dr Barnardo didn't laugh. He turned back to Vic.

'Where are *you* going to sleep tonight?' he asked gently.

She shrugged. 'Under one of the arches of London Bridge, I expect.'

Albert shivered.

Mr Browne cleared his throat.

'Dr Barnardo, on the matter of your Girls' Home in the village of Barkingside. You said that it can open as soon as there is enough money to pay for all the maids and cooks. You asked for my help and I said that I would give you my answer today.'

'You did, sir.'

'Well, doctor, I will *give* you – not lend you – the required money on three conditions.'

'And what are they, Mr Browne?' asked Dr Barnardo eagerly.

'That you will open it tonight. That you will accept regular sums from me to pay for the first occupant until she can earn a living. And that this first waif will be Miss Victoria Wells.'

Dr Barnardo removed his spectacles and wiped his grey eyes.

'I agree to your terms. Thank you and God bless you, sir.'

Then he went on: 'It will be a privilege to have such a brave young lady as my first

resident. She'll inspire all the others. A home in the Essex countryside, under Christian influences, with education and training, will be the first step towards a better life for her, God willing.'

'One thing's for sure, Vic,' said Albert, smiling. 'You'll never have to be a chimney child again.'

AUTHOR'S NOTE

Dr Barnardo did get help from banking families but the Brownes were not real people. Neither were the other characters.

The ancient scandal of the climbing boys was finally ended in 1875, two years after the time of this story. The great reformer Lord Shaftesbury believed that in London itself the practice had already stopped and, on the whole, it had. But near Cambridge, George Brewster, 11, died after sweeping an asylum flue. So Shaftesbury got an Act passed strengthening the existing laws. Under the Act, sweeps had to be licensed and anyone breaking the law was banned from the trade. And, most important of all, the police were ordered to enforce those laws. So the climbing boys didn't climb any more. Neither did the girls.

Dr Barnardo created Britain's biggest children's charity. Under his emigration scheme, thousands of children were sent to Canada and, later, Australia, too. He opened many homes in Britain. However, he believed that caring for children in the community, as opposed to an institution, prepared them better for living in the real world. The people now in charge of Barnardo's agree with this and the charity no longer runs orphanages. Instead, children live with families or in council homes. But Barnardo's does help 30,000 young people every year in 250 services throughout the UK. There are also independent Barnardo organizations in the Irish Republic, Australia and New Zealand.

PLACES TO VISIT

Cherished Chimneys, Station St, Longport, Burslem, Staffs.
Climbing boy and chimney-pot museum: memorabilia, tapes.

Museum of Childhood, Sudbury Hall, Sudbury, Derbyshire
How children lived, including sweeps. Climb the chimney!

Isle of Wight Wax Works, High St, Brading, Isle of Wight
Look down on Valentine Gray in the chimney! (Valentine died from
blows to the head inflicted by his master, who was convicted of
manslaughter and fined one shilling.)

Gray Monument, Church Litten, Newport, Isle of Wight
In memory of Valentine Gray.

'Eros' (Shaftesbury Memorial), Piccadilly Circus, London
Lord Shaftesbury's Act ended the climbing boy system.

Stepney Causeway, London: blue plaque
Site of Barnardo's home for destitute boys.

Barnardo's, Tanners Lane, Barkingside, Ilford, Essex
Cottages, Barnardo grave and soon a heritage centre.

Ragged School Museum, Copperfield Rd, Bow, London
Barnardo school – attend a lesson. East End displays.

**Bethnal Green Museum of Childhood,
Cambridge Heath Road, Bethnal Green, London**
Costumes, toys, etc.

Museum of London, London Wall
Newgate doors, cab, kitchen, shops, schoolroom, costume.

Central Criminal Court, The Old Bailey, London
Site of Newgate. Prison stones in the court walls.

Madame Tussaud's, Marylebone Rd, London
Newgate gallows, bell, condemned-cell door. Furniture.

St Bartholomew's Hospital, West Smithfield, London
London's oldest hospital, founded 1123. Museum, North Wing:
hospital's history, including Victorian toys.

**Museum in Docklands, W. India Quay,
opposite Canary Wharf, London**
Opens Year 2000. Listed warehouse showing Thames history.

River trips via Docklands, London (River Trip Line: 0891-505-471)
Commentaries: riverside history and old docks' new role.

Staffordshire County Museum, Shugborough Hall, nr Milford
Butler's quarters, kitchen, schoolroom, cab, carriages.
'Life of a Child' gallery opens 1999.

Museum of Childhood, High Street, Edinburgh
Medicine, books, clothes, etc.

Rochester Sweeps Festival, Rochester, Kent
Sweeps Parade, May Day Bank Holiday. Be a climbing boy!

Geffrye Museum, Kingsland Rd, Shoreditch, London
Period rooms. Drama, music, etc., bring museum to life.

House of Detention, Clerkenwell Close, Clerkenwell, London
Guided tour of underground prison's tunnels and cells.

**Florence Nightingale Museum,
St Thomas's Hospital, Lambeth, London**
Nursing history. Living-room and slum cottage re-created.

**Victoria and Albert Museum,
Cromwell Rd, South Kensington, London**
Furniture, artefacts, fashionable clothes.

London Transport Museum, The Piazza, Covent Garden, London
Horse-buses/trams. Public transport history on video.

Castle Museum (former Female and Debtors' Prisons), York
Reconstructed street: cobbles, shops, cab. Clothes, etc.

Towneley Hall, nr Burnley, Lancs.
Mansion showing how people lived – furniture, artefacts.

Abbey House Museum, Abbey Rd, Kirkstall, Leeds
Streets, shops. Sitting-room, fireplaces, clothes, toys.

**Cambridge and County Folk Museum (former inn),
Castle St, Cambridge**
Sweeps' brushes, open hearth, cooking, toys, trades, etc.

Museum of Costume, Assembly Rooms, Bennett St, Bath
Rich people's clothes.

Linley Sambourne House, 18 Stafford Terrace, Kensington, London
Late-Victorian middle-class town house with the artist's furnishings and
Water Babies climbing boy pictures.

'How We Lived Then' Museum of Shops, Eastbourne, E. Sussex
Shops, rooms: 100,000+ exhibits collected over 40 years.